DETECTIVE TRICKS
YOU CAN DO

Written by Judith Conaway
Illustrated by Renzo Barto

Troll Associates

Library of Congress Cataloging in Publication Data

Conaway, Judith, (date)
    Detective tricks you can do.

    Summary: Follows two young detectives through an
investigation and introduces such tricks and techniques
as mirror writing, codes, invisible ink, fingerprinting,
and other tools of the trade.
    1. Creative activities and seat work—Juvenile
literature.   2. Detectives—Juvenile literature.
3. Tricks—Juvenile literature.   [1. Detectives.
2. Tricks]   I. Barto, Renzo, ill.   II. Title.
GV1203.C578   1986   793.5   85-28881
ISBN 0-8167-0672-7 (lib. bdg.)
ISBN 0-8167-0673-5 (pbk.)

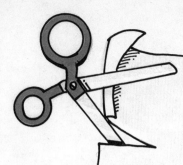

CONTENTS

MRS. MONTAGUE'S MESSAGE

Becky and Bill were blue. They were at "B and B Snoops," their detective agency. But the phone had not rung all day. Suddenly, there was a knock at the door.

A woman entered. She looked puzzled. "I am Mrs. Montague," she said. "My housekeeper found this note today. Can you help me figure the message out?"

Becky laughed. "You can figure that out if you reflect on it," she said, taking a small mirror out of her purse.

Can you read the message?
Becky has given you a clue on how to do it.

Here's how:
Hold this message up to a mirror, and you'll be able to read the "backwards" writing.

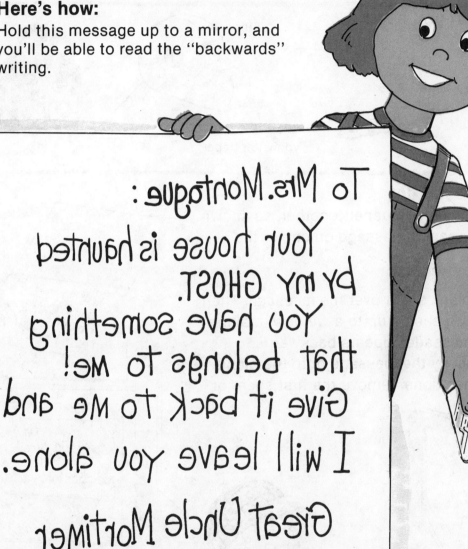

To Mrs. Montague:
Your house is haunted
by my GHOST.
You have something
that belongs to me!
Give it back to me and
I will leave you alone.

Great Uncle Mortimer

(Here's what the message to Mrs. Montague said: *To Mrs. Montague: Your house is haunted by my GHOST. You have something that belongs to me! Give it back to me and I will leave you alone. Great Uncle Mortimer*)

"A mirror," said Mrs. Montague. "How clever!"
"Your ghost is a very clever one," said Bill. "But we're smart, too. First, we'll write a message in return."
Turn the page to find out how.

5

MIRROR WRITING

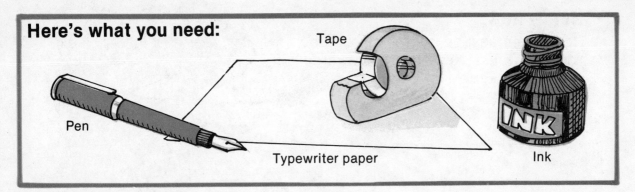

Here's what you need:

Pen

Tape

Typewriter paper

Ink

Here's what you do:

1 Tape two sheets of paper together, as shown. Write your secret message on one of the sheets.

2 Fold the blank sheet over the message. Then hold the two sheets up to a window, making sure the message appears backwards. Carefully copy the message onto the blank sheet. When done, remove the first sheet of paper.

3 You now have a message written in secret code. To read it, hold it up to a mirror.

Here is the message that Becky and Bill wrote to Mrs. Montague's ghost.

6

COLOR-BAR CODE

The next day, Mrs. Montague returned. "The ghost answered our message," she said. "This came today."

"It's a color-bar code," Bill said. "We have the key to figure it out right here."

Can you read the message?

To read the message, match the color bars shown in the note to the letters shown below in the code.

(Answer: *I WANT YOUR TREASURE.*)

SUBSTITUTION CODES

Later that afternoon, Becky and Bill returned to their office. They found yet *another* message.

"It looks like it's written in a substitution code," said Becky. "Let's figure it out!"

A substitution code is a code in which letters are replaced by numbers or symbols. In the simplest code, you substitute numbers for letters, as shown on the top of page 9.

13-25 20-18-5-1-19.21-185,
3-1-13-5 6-18-15-13
3-8-9-14-1. 9-20 9-19
8-9-4-4-5-14 14-5-1-18
25-15-21-18 7-1-18-4-5-14
23-1-12-12 .
7-18-5-1-20 21-14-3-12-5
13-15-18-20-9-13-5-18

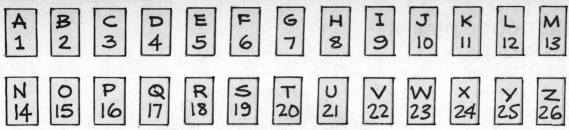

Use this code to read the message on page 8.

Here's an easy way to invent your own code:

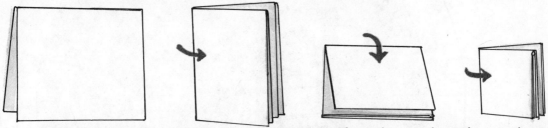

1 Fold a sheet of paper in half...then in half again...and again...and one last time. Unfold the paper. You should have sixteen rectangles. Next, do the same to another sheet of paper.

2 Print each letter of the alphabet, one to a rectangle. Below each letter, draw a different symbol. Use the ones shown here or make up some of your own.

3 Cut apart the rectangles. Shuffle the cards and try to memorize the code.

4 One way to write a message is to make several copies of each card. Arrange the cards so they spell out the words of your message. Then copy down the symbols, in order, on a sheet of paper.

(Answer: *My treasure came from China. It is hidden near your garden wall. Great Uncle Mortimer*)

POCKET CODE DIALER

Here's an easy way to use substitution codes. All you do is turn the dial!

Here's what you need:

Construction paper

Compass

Pencil

Black marker

Metal fastener

Scissors

Writing paper

Here's what you do:

1 Copy these two circles onto two different colors of paper.

2 Print the numbers on the smaller circle and write the alphabet on the other circle.

3 Cut out the two circles. Make a small hole in the center of each circle.

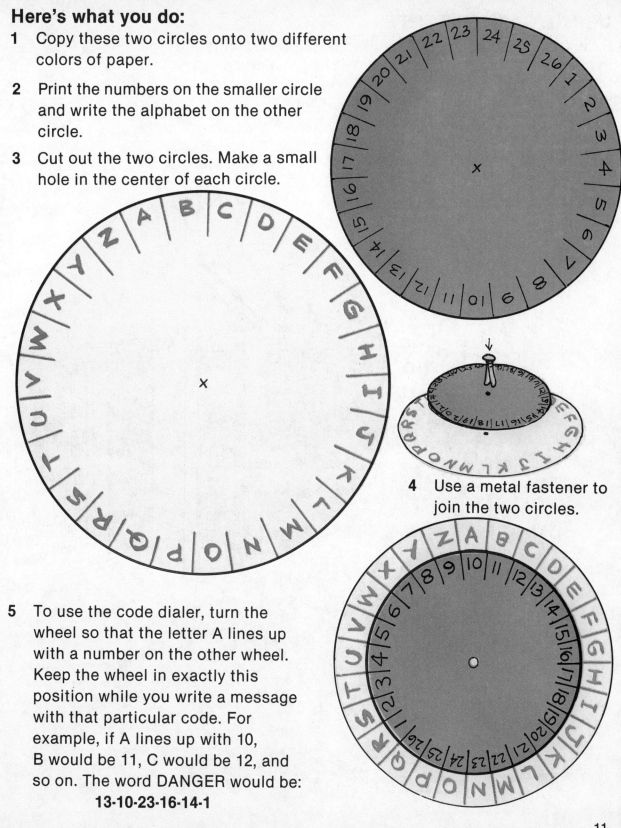

4 Use a metal fastener to join the two circles.

5 To use the code dialer, turn the wheel so that the letter A lines up with a number on the other wheel. Keep the wheel in exactly this position while you write a message with that particular code. For example, if A lines up with 10, B would be 11, C would be 12, and so on. The word DANGER would be:
13-10-23-16-14-1

UP THE GARDEN PATH

Early the next morning, Bill and Becky met Mrs. Montague in her garden to search for treasure. They dug and dug, but found nothing!

"It's no use," said Bill. "There's no treasure."

"I'm afraid my Great Uncle Mortimer must have made a mistake," said Mrs. Montague.

"Unless," said Becky, "it *wasn't* a mistake. Maybe there is no ghost.
Maybe someone just wanted to keep us out of the house all this time!"
"Tell us," said Bill, "where do you keep your most valuable things, Mrs.
Montague?"
"Why, in the library safe," she answered.
"Quick!" said Becky. "Let's go!"

Once inside, Mrs. Montague opened the safe and took out a
box of jewelry.
"Oh no," Mrs. Montague said. "My great-grandmother's pearls—some are
missing. And this ring used to have four diamonds, not just two. Someone
has been robbing my jewels, bit by bit."
"Don't worry," said Bill. "We'll find the thief. Come on, Becky. Let's test
for fingerprints."

FINGERPRINTING KIT

Becky and Bill are fingerprinting experts. It may take you a little practice to learn this art—the secret is a light touch.

Here's what you need:

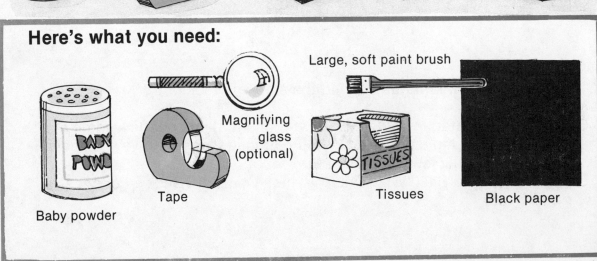

Baby powder

Tape

Magnifying glass (optional)

Large, soft paint brush

Tissues

Black paper

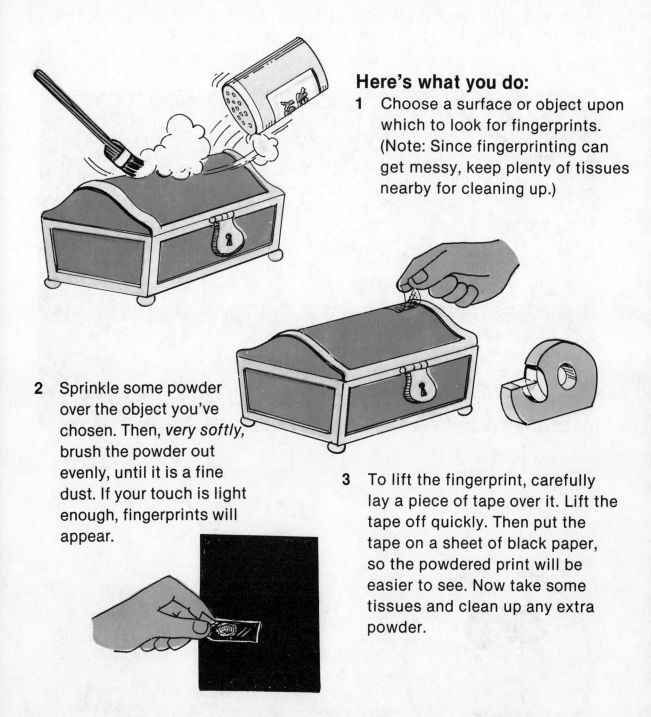

Here's what you do:

1 Choose a surface or object upon which to look for fingerprints. (Note: Since fingerprinting can get messy, keep plenty of tissues nearby for cleaning up.)

2 Sprinkle some powder over the object you've chosen. Then, *very softly,* brush the powder out evenly, until it is a fine dust. If your touch is light enough, fingerprints will appear.

3 To lift the fingerprint, carefully lay a piece of tape over it. Lift the tape off quickly. Then put the tape on a sheet of black paper, so the powdered print will be easier to see. Now take some tissues and clean up any extra powder.

Look carefully at the fingerprints with a magnifying glass, if you have one. It's true! No two people's fingerprints are exactly alike. Your fingerprints are even more personal than your name!

THE PERSONAL TOUCH

Becky and Bill found Mrs. Montague's fingerprints on the safe—*plus* two other sets of prints. So there are two suspects in the case:

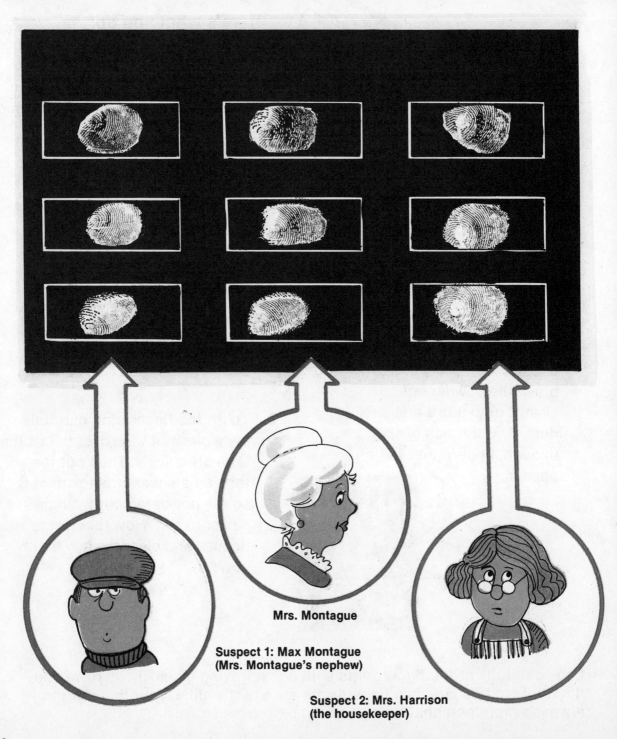

Mrs. Montague

**Suspect 1: Max Montague
(Mrs. Montague's nephew)**

**Suspect 2: Mrs. Harrison
(the housekeeper)**

FINGERPRINT NOTEBOOK FILE

For every case, Bill and Becky keep track of the fingerprints of all their suspects. With this fingerprint file, so can you!

Here's what you need:

Ink pad

Pen

Small notebook

Tissues

Here's what you do:

1 Gather the fingerprints of your suspects by pressing each one's thumb on an ink pad.

Then press the thumb onto a page of the notebook. (Keep tissues handy for cleaning up.)

2 Use your notebook to study and compare your suspects' fingerprints.

DETECTIVE KIT

"So, we've got two suspects," said Becky to Bill. "Mrs. Montague's nephew—Max Montague; and Mrs. Harrison—the housekeeper."

"We'll have to follow both of them," said Bill. "This calls for using our B and B Snoops Detective Kit."

On the next few pages, you'll find directions for making some of the tools in the detective's kit.

SEE-AND-SPY DETECTIVE MAGAZINE

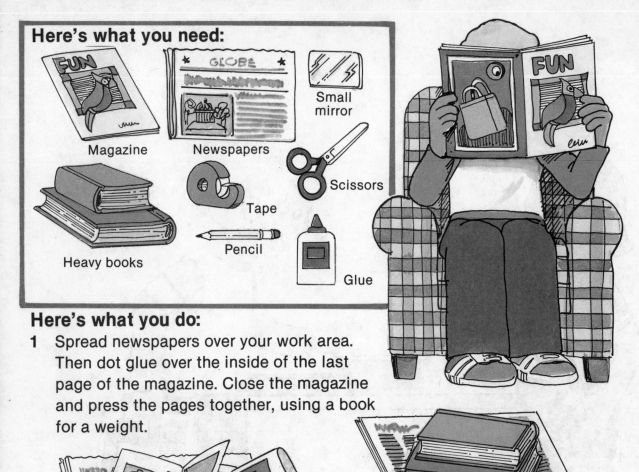

Here's what you need:

Magazine

Newspapers

Small mirror

Scissors

Tape

Heavy books

Pencil

Glue

Here's what you do:

1   Spread newspapers over your work area. Then dot glue over the inside of the last page of the magazine. Close the magazine and press the pages together, using a book for a weight.

2   Open the magazine to the glued pages. Cut out a small circle for a peephole, as shown. Tape a mirror to the opposite page.

3   To spy with your magazine, use the peephole to see everything happening in front of you. Pretend to read the magazine, so no one suspects.

4 To watch what's happening behind you, look in the mirror, while holding the magazine as though you are reading.

REARVIEW DRINKING GLASS

Here's another tool in the
B and B Snoops Detective Kit.
It's perfect for sitting in a
restaurant and watching the
action *behind* you.

Here's what you need:

Tape

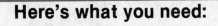

Small round mirror

Small paper cup

Glue

Large paper cup

Here's what you do:

1 Put some glue inside the bottom of the smaller cup. Press the small round mirror into the glue, mirror side facing up. Let the glue dry.

2 Place the smaller cup inside the larger cup. Tape the two cups together, as shown.

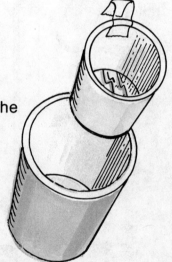

Tape

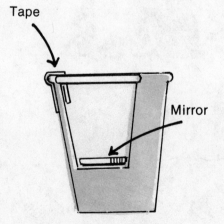

Mirror

3 To use this tool, pretend you're drinking from the cup. Hold the smaller cup steady with your thumb. You will be able to see behind you by looking in the mirror. Practice looking natural— you don't want anyone to detect the detective!

WALKIE-TALKIE

A walkie-talkie is another good detective's tool. With it, you can send and receive messages over a distance without making too much noise.

Here's what you need:

2 Paper cups

Toothpicks

Scissors

Ruler

Nylon string

Here's what you do:

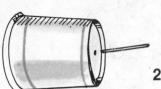

1. Punch a hole in the bottom of each cup with a toothpick. Make the hole just big enough for the nylon string to pass through.

2. Cut a piece of nylon string that is 10-15 feet long.

3. Thread a cup to each end of the string, as shown. Tie each end of the string to the center of a toothpick. Pull each cup back along the string until the toothpick catches in the bottom of the cup. The toothpicks will hold the string in place inside the cups and will pick up the vibrations of your voice.

4. Try out your walkie-talkie by stretching out the string. Talk into one of the cups, while a friend puts the other cup to his or her ear. See how softly you can speak and still be heard.

BODY SIGNALS

Every detective needs to know how to send a secret message. Body signals are small movements you make up to mean certain things.
Here are some ideas:

Crossing your legs could mean...*I think they suspect something!*

A tug on the ear could mean...*Careful, someone's listening!*

Scratching your head could mean...*Go get help.*

A rub on the back of the neck could mean...*Someone's behind you!*

A big yawn could mean...*Quick! Let's get out of here.*

Clearing your throat could mean...*Watch out! Danger!*

Passing your hand over your eyes could mean...*We're being watched.*

Of course, it's fun to make up some of your own signals. Sit down with a friend and come up with some body signals and their meanings. Write down your ideas, making a copy for each of you. That way you can both memorize the signals. Practice making the signals look as natural as possible so no one will suspect.

INVISIBLE INK

One of Bill and Becky's favorite ways to write secret messages is with invisible ink. You can, too. Here's how.

Here's what you need:

White paper

Lemon

Knife

Cup

Toothpick

100-Watt light bulb

Here's what you do:

1 Carefully slice a lemon in half. (If you're not allowed to use a knife by yourself, ask a grownup for help.)

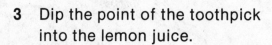

2 Squeeze the juice into a cup.

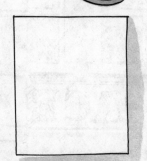

3 Dip the point of the toothpick into the lemon juice.

4 Now write your message on a sheet of white paper, using the toothpick as a "pen" and the lemon juice as your "ink." When the juice dries, the message will be invisible.

5 To make the message appear, carefully hold the letter near the lighted bulb. As the heat from the bulb warms up the paper, the lemon juice heats up faster and starts to turn brown. Soon the message appears.

DISGUISE GLASSES

A must for every detective is a good disguise. These glasses will help!

Here's what you need:

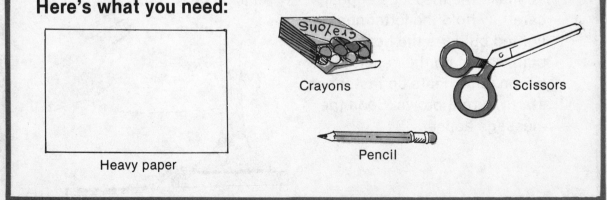

Heavy paper

Crayons

Scissors

Pencil

Here's what you do:

1 Fold a sheet of paper in half, as shown.

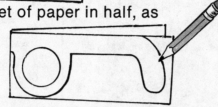

2 Copy the pattern for the glasses (shown at right) onto the paper. Be sure the fold of the paper lines up with the part of the glasses that fits over your nose.

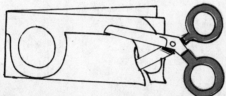

3 Cut out the pattern—cut through both sides of the folded paper. Carefully cut out the eye holes.

4 Unfold your glasses. Use crayons to color them.

Fold ➞   Fold

5 Fold the two hooked ear pieces back. Put them on and see how you look.

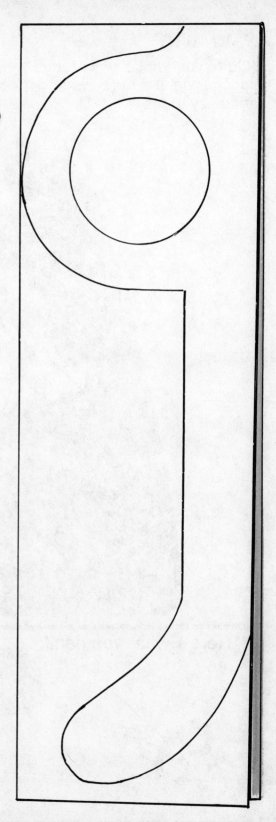

YARN WIG

Add to your disguise with this special wig. It's fun to wear and easy to make.

Here's what you need:

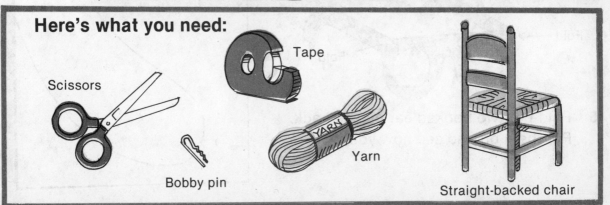

Scissors

Tape

Bobby pin

Yarn

Straight-backed chair

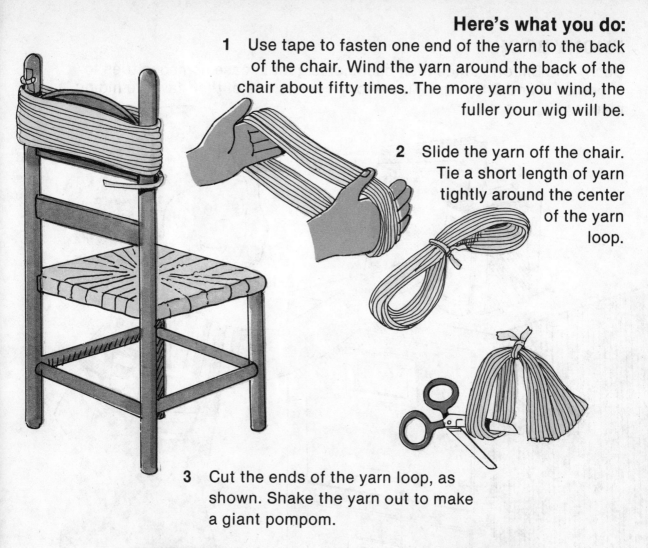

Here's what you do:

1 Use tape to fasten one end of the yarn to the back of the chair. Wind the yarn around the back of the chair about fifty times. The more yarn you wind, the fuller your wig will be.

2 Slide the yarn off the chair. Tie a short length of yarn tightly around the center of the yarn loop.

3 Cut the ends of the yarn loop, as shown. Shake the yarn out to make a giant pompom.

4 Trim the wig as shown above, or braid it. Use a bobby pin to attach the wig to your own hair.

PHONY BOOK

Becky and Bill often hide their case notes, just in case someone tries to snoop on B and B Snoops. This phony book is one of their favorite hiding places.

Here's what you need:

Thin, book-sized box with fold-down lid

Glue

Newspapers

Ruler

Scissors

Pencil

Markers

Construction paper and white paper

Here's what you do:

1 Cut a strip of white paper long enough to fit around three of the thin sides of the box. The strip should be wide enough to completely cover the thin sides.

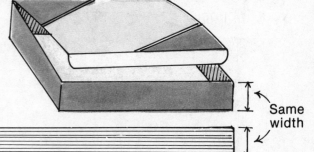

Same width

2 Draw thin lines along the strip to look like the "pages" of your book.

3 Spread newspapers over the area where you're working to keep it clean. Fold the strip to fit around the book and glue it in place.

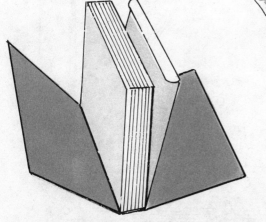

4 Cut a sheet of paper for the cover of the book. It should be large enough to cover the remaining three sides of the box. Fold it around the book.

5 Now place the cover flat and decorate it. Position the cover around the box and glue in place.

6 Your book is ready to use as a hiding place for your secret papers.

"WANTED" POSTERS

These posters are a funny way to use any extra school pictures of yourself and your friends.

Here's what you need:

Posterboard or construction paper

Glue

Photos

Crayons or markers

Scissors

Ruler

Here's what you do:

1 Use crayons or markers to write the word "Wanted" on your poster.

2 Below, write a short description of the "crime." See the ideas on the following pages —or make up some funny crimes of your own.

3 Glue the photo to the poster.

4 If you like, choose a disguise from pages 40-41. Draw it on the photo. Or you can draw the disguise on construction paper and cut out the pieces. Then glue the disguise to the photo.

5 Write in the name of the "criminal."

6 When all the glue has dried, color and decorate your poster. It's ready to hang up!

WANTED

name _____

ROGUES' GALLERY

Here are some famous "criminals." Can you think of any more funny "crimes" for your wanted posters?

WANTED

FOR SMUGGLING SNAILS

name _____

description:
  last seen hanging
    around beaches.

WANTED

FOR TELLING BAD JOKES

name _____

description:
  Hangs around the
Lunch Room on Tuesday.

WANTED

FOR
SLURPING SOUP

name _____

description:
carries two bowls of soup
at all times.
Very dangerous!

WANTED

FOR
IMPERSONATING A STUDENT

name _____

description:
Last seen near the
school library two years ago.

DAFFY DISGUISES

Here are some ideas for disguises to add to the photos in your wanted posters. Modify them to fit the size of the photo you're using.

CLANGING ALARM

This special alarm can warn you if you're being snooped on!

Here's what you need:

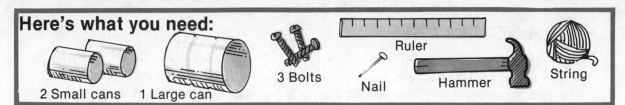

2 Small cans 1 Large can 3 Bolts Nail Ruler Hammer String

Here's what you do:

1 Carefully wash the empty tin cans and remove the labels. Dry the cans well.

2 With a hammer and nail, make a hole in the bottom of each can. (If you're not allowed to use a hammer by yourself, ask a grownup for help.)

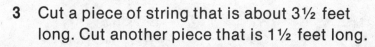

3 Cut a piece of string that is about 3½ feet long. Cut another piece that is 1½ feet long.

4 Tie a bolt to one end of the long piece of string. Thread the string up through the inside of the large can. Pull the string through until the bolt catches against the hole.

5 Find the center of the short piece of string. Attach the midpoint of the short string to the long string, about 3½ inches above the large can. Tie it tightly in a double knot.

6 Thread a small can to one end of the short string. Then tie a bolt to the end of the string to hold the can in place. Do the same with the second small can on the other end of the short string.

7 Choose a door or window you wish to snoop-proof. Tie your alarm to the inside of the window-latch or doorknob. If someone tries to enter the room, the cans will clang against each other, and you will be warned.

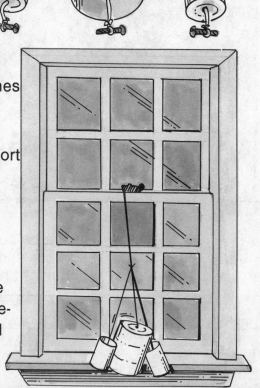

SUMMING UP A CASE

Summing up a case is probably the hardest detective work of all. Why? Because you must use your *brains* to do it! Read below to see how Becky and Bill have put together all the facts in the case of Mrs. Montague's ghost.

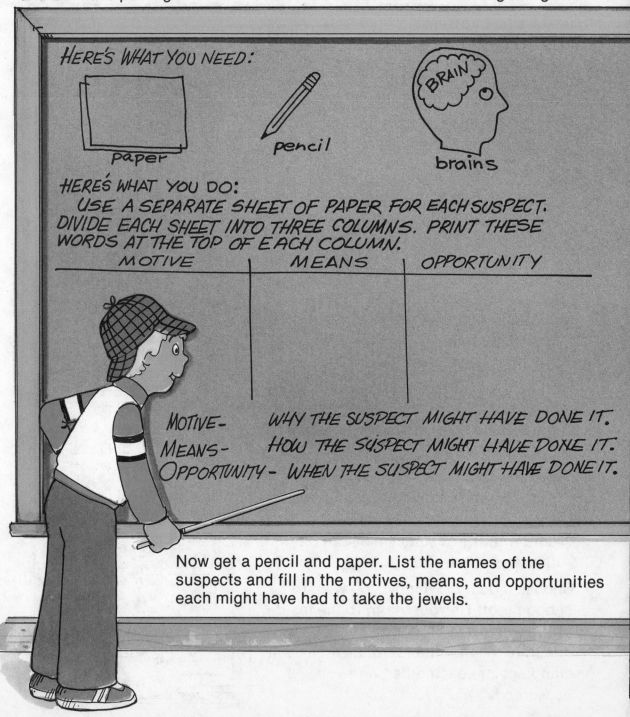

HERE'S WHAT YOU NEED:

paper

pencil

BRAIN

brains

HERE'S WHAT YOU DO:
USE A SEPARATE SHEET OF PAPER FOR EACH SUSPECT. DIVIDE EACH SHEET INTO THREE COLUMNS. PRINT THESE WORDS AT THE TOP OF EACH COLUMN.

MOTIVE	MEANS	OPPORTUNITY

MOTIVE— WHY THE SUSPECT MIGHT HAVE DONE IT.
MEANS— HOW THE SUSPECT MIGHT HAVE DONE IT.
OPPORTUNITY— WHEN THE SUSPECT MIGHT HAVE DONE IT.

Now get a pencil and paper. List the names of the suspects and fill in the motives, means, and opportunities each might have had to take the jewels.

WHO DID IT?

Which suspect is more likely to be the thief? For the answer, read on.

MOTIVE	MEANS	OPPORTUNITY
MAX MONTAGUE: WORKS AS A WAITER. EARNS VERY LITTLE CASH. SEEMS TO SPEND A LOT. COMPLAINS THAT HE WOULD BE RICH IF ONLY HIS AUNT WOULD GIVE HIM MONEY.	LIVED IN THE MONTAGUE HOUSE AS A CHILD. COULD HAVE LEARNED THE SAFE COMBINATION FROM HIS FATHER.	CAN'T GET AT THE SAFE UNLESS MRS. MONTAGUE IS OUT OF THE HOUSE. AUNT DOESN'T LET HIM IN THE HOUSE.
MRS. HARRISON: SEEMS TO BE A CAREFUL PERSON WHO SAVES HER MONEY. SEEMS TO LIKE MRS. MONTAGUE AND IS HAPPY WORKING FOR HER.	COULD HAVE LEARNED THE SAFE COMBINATION BY SPYING ON MRS. MONTAGUE OR SEARCHING HER PAPERS. ALMOST NEVER LEAVES THE HOUSE.	CAN GET AT THE SAFE ANYTIME.

THE GHOST GETS GRABBED

The next day, Bill and Becky called the police to let them know *who* they thought might be taking Mrs. Montague's jewels.

Then, pretending to leave the house, Mrs. Montague and the two detectives were joined by Officer Smedley. All four of them circled back and hid in the library where the safe is kept. Soon the detectives heard footsteps. Someone had entered the room. *Click, click* went the lock on the safe. Officer Smedley jumped out and surprised the thief. It was none other than Max Montague!

"Thanks, Becky and Bill," said Officer Smedley. "We couldn't have caught the thief without you!"

Becky and Bill just beamed. They had tackled another baffling case and solved it! Now *you're* ready to do some detective work of your own—good luck!